Little Goblins Ten

By **Pamela Jane**

Illustrated by **Jane Manning**

SCHOLASTIC INC.
New York Toronto London Auckland
Sydney Mexico City New Delhi Hong Kong

Over in the forest
    Where the trees hide the sun
Lived a big mommy monster
    And her little monster one.

"Scare!" said the mommy;

"I scare," said the one.

So he scared and he scampered

Where the trees hide the sun.

Over in the forest
　　Where spooks shout, "Boo!"
Lived a pale daddy ghost
　　And his little ghosties two.

"Haunt!" cried the daddy;
    "We haunt," cried the two.
So they hid and they haunted
    Where spooks shout, "Boo!"

Over in the forest
 Near a gnarled oak tree
Lived an old mother zombie
 And her little zombies three.

"Stare!" said the mommy;
 "We stare," said the three.
So they stared all together
 Near the gnarled oak tree.

Over in the forest
  Where the fierce winds roar
Lived a gray father werewolf
  And his little wolvies four.

"Howl!" said the father;
  "We howl," said the four.
So they howled and they growled
  Where the fierce winds roar.

Over in the forest
  Where the shadows come alive
Lived an old mother mummy
  And her little mummies five.

"Moan!" said the mother;
  "We moan," said the five.
So they moaned and they groaned
  Where the shadows come alive.

Over in the forest
    In a hovel made of sticks
Lived an old mother witch
    And her little witches six.

"Cackle!" screeched the mother;
    "We cackle," screeched the six.
So they crowed and they cackled
    In the hovel made of sticks.

Over in the forest
   In a mossy green heaven
Lived a scaly father dragon
   And his little dragons seven.

"Breathe!" said the father;
 "We breathe," said the seven.
So they breathed flames of fire
 In the mossy green heaven.

Over in the forest
By the graveyard gate
Lived a bony father skeleton
And his little skellies eight.

"Rattle!" said the father;
  "We rattle," said the eight.
So they rattled and they ran
  By the graveyard gate.

Over in the forest
    Near a tall dark pine
Lived a furry mother bat
    And her little batties nine.

"Swoop!" cried the mother;
    "We swoop," cried the nine.
So they swooped in the shadows
    Near the tall dark pine.

Over in the forest
In a deep green glen
Lived an old father goblin
And his little goblins ten.

"Leap!" said the father;
  "We leap," said the ten.
So they laughed and they leaped
  In the deep green glen.

Over in the forest
    Where the trees hide the sun
The big mommy called
    To her little monster one.

"Trick or treat?" asked the mommy;
"Treat!" cried the one.
So they skipped off together
For some Halloween fun!

To my mother and father, who read to me
before I understood the words
—P.J.

To Mike and Judy, with love
—J.M.

ISBN 978-0-545-49299-7

Text copyright © 2011 by Pamela Jane.
Illustrations copyright © 2011 by Jane Manning.
All rights reserved. Published by Scholastic Inc., 557 Broadway, New York, NY 10012,
by arrangement with HarperCollins Children's Books, a division of HarperCollins Publishers.
SCHOLASTIC and associated logos are trademarks and/or registered trademarks of Scholastic Inc.

12 11 10 9 8 7 6 5 4 3 2 1   12 13 14 15 16 17/0

Printed in the U.S.A.   08

First Scholastic printing, September 2012

Typography by Jennifer Rozbruch